Chapter One

One morning Shelley's teacher Ms Garland came into the classroom and handed each of the children a plain white envelope. Inside each envelope was a piece of paper. On Shelley's was written:

My name is Tomi Wong.
I'm from Ningbo in China.
I'm your new pen-pal.

"Today," said Ms Garland, when everyone had had time to read their piece of paper, "we're going to learn how to write letters to our new pen-pals."

A cheer went up in the classroom.

"Now, how many of you have written a letter before?"

One or two of the children waved their hands in the air.

# All the Way
# from China

For Kate, Sarah, David and Aoife

Published 1998 by
Poolbeg Press Ltd
123 Baldoyle Industrial Estate
Dublin 13, Ireland

Text © Pat Boran 1998
Illustrations © Stewart Curry 1998

Reprinted November 1998

The moral right of the author has been asserted.

**The Arts Council**
An Chomhairle Ealaíon

A catalogue record for this book is available from the British Library.

ISBN 1 85371 853 X

Illustrations by Stewart Curry
Cover design by Poolbeg Group Services Ltd
Set by Poolbeg Group Services Ltd in Times 16/25
Printed by The Guernsey Press Ltd,
Vale, Guernsey, Channel Islands.

As Ms Garland began to describe what a letter should look like, Shelley, who always sat on her own, took her books and slipped quietly down to the back of the classroom, hoping no one had noticed her.

"The first thing to do," said Ms Garland, "is to write your own address on the top of the page on the right-hand side. That way the person you are writing to will know where you are and will be able to write back. For example, when the President of Ireland writes a letter, the top right-hand corner looks like this."

She took a piece of chalk and wrote on the blackboard:

"Now, can each of you please write your own address in the same way?"

Shelley turned over a new page in her copybook and wrote:

Apartment 14
27 Alder Road
Dublin 5

"Very good," said Ms Garland, coming around to make sure everyone had understood. "Now, the next thing to do is to write today's date underneath." Again she turned to the blackboard and wrote:

Monday 5th February

"After that, move down a couple of lines and, this time at the *left-hand* side of the page, write:

and the name of the person you are writing to. Does everybody understand?"

Shelley moved down a few lines, went to the left-hand side of the page and wrote:

Dear Tomi Wong

"Now," said Ms Garland, "beginning on the next line below, you can write just about anything you like. And, when you've finished, I'll collect all the letters and send them for you. All you have to do is to make sure you put your pen-pal's name on the envelope. But remember that your new pen-pal doesn't know anything about you, so you might like to tell something about yourself and where you live. All right now, off you go."

At that, all of the other children put their heads down and began to write furiously. Some of them were even concentrating so much that their tongues stuck out of the sides of their mouths.

"Is there anything the matter, Shelley?" asked Ms Garland, coming down to find Shelley staring at a page with nothing written on it except her address, the date and Dear Tomi Wong. "It's not like you to run out of ideas."

Shelley looked up sadly. "I don't know what to write, Miss," she said. "My life is so ordinary that no one would want to hear about it. I wish I still lived in the countryside. Something exciting always happened there."

Ms Garland knew that Shelley was not very happy since she had moved to the city with her mother, but she also knew that maybe Shelley just needed some encouragement.

"Now, Shelley," she said, "you must try to remember that all lives are full of extraordinary things. It's just that people forget how extraordinary they are because they see them day after day."

Shelley had to think about this for a minute, so Ms Garland continued.

"Imagine that you wrote a letter to someone who knew nothing at all about you or where you lived," she said.

"You mean like Tomi Wong?" said Shelley.

"Yes," said Ms Garland. "Like Tomi Wong. Imagine how exciting that would be."

"But I don't speak Chinese!" said Shelley.

Ms Garland smiled. "That's all right," she said. "Tomi's half-Irish. That's why the first half of his name is in English, more or less. So, what do you think? Will you write to him?"

"I suppose so," said Shelley after a while.

"Excellent," said Ms Garland. "In that case, I'll leave you to it."

By the end of the class, however though some of the other children were showing off pages and pages of letters they had written, Shelley had managed to add only one sentence to her letter so that it now read:

Apartment 14
27 Alder Road
Dublin 5
Monday 5th February

Dear Tomi Wong,
My name is Shelley Watters.

"Maybe you'll be able to do it when you get home," said Ms Garland, coming down to Shelley's desk when the final bell had sounded.

"Yes," said Shelley, but she did not feel very hopeful.

## Chapter Two

That evening Shelley's mother didn't have to go to work at the hospital, so instead they watched a film on television. The film was about an old woman who was writing her first book. There were so many pages of the book that she had to keep them in a shoe box.

"We were writing letters today," said Shelley during the advertisements. "It's hard."

"Lots of people find it hard," said her mother.

"You mean like Dad?" asked Shelley. "Is that why he hardly ever writes any more, except at Christmas and on my birthday?"

Her mother was silent for a minute.

"Yes," she said. "I suppose so. On the other hand, you've always been good at writing, Shelley. Just let your imagination go."

Shelley liked to hear her mother say
things like that. So, when the film was
over she went to her room, took out her
pen and copybook and sat down before
the letter again.

But the more she looked at it the more difficult it became to think of anything interesting to write about Dublin. So she turned over to a new page and wrote:

Meadow View
Tralee
County Kerry
Monday 5th February

She looked at her old address for a long time. She thought about the places where she used to play with her friends, and the places she used to visit with her father and mother when they were not busy working. Then she continued:

Dear Tomi Wong,

My name is Shelley Watters. I am eight years of age. I am not really very good at writing letters. In fact, this is my first time. I would like to tell you about my favourite animals. On the farm where I live there are ducks, cows, chickens and even sheep . . . Are there sheep on the farms in China? What kind of food do you eat? My mother says everyone eats rice. Is that true? Write and tell me all about your country.

Yours,

Shelley Watters

When she had finished the letter she read it over again to make sure there were no spelling mistakes. Then she put her pen and copybook aside, climbed into bed, and turned out the light. Outside the traffic continued to pass noisily until she fell asleep.

## Chapter Three

In school the next morning Shelley handed the envelope with the letter in it to Ms Garland.

"I see you've already sealed it," said Ms Garland.

"Yes," said Shelley, hoping Ms Garland wouldn't want to open it and check the spelling. She didn't want Ms Garland to see that she had pretended to be living in Kerry still.

"In that case," said Ms Garland with a smile, "just write Tomi's name on the envelope and I'll send it off for you after school."

So Shelley took up her pen and wrote Tomi's name on the envelope of the first letter she'd ever written.

"Now we'll just have to wait and see," said Ms Garland.

Shelley didn't have to wait for very long. In fact, even though China is more than 5,000 miles away, and it must take a long time for even a very fast plane to get there, when Shelley walked into the classroom on Friday morning Ms Garland met her with another envelope.

This one, however, had something written on it in different coloured inks.

"For me?" asked Shelley, full of surprise.

Ms Garland nodded. "For you," she said.
And she handed the envelope to Shelley.

Shelley felt a little embarrassed, but she said nothing. Instead she took the envelope and ran down to her desk at the back of the class, almost tripping over the legs of one of her dozy classmates.

When she was sitting down she opened the envelope and took out the letter. Like her name on the envelope, the letter itself was written in different colours.

Ningbo
Zhejiang
China
Wednesday 7th February

Dear Shelley Watters,
My name is Tomi Wong. I am 8 and three-quarters. I live with my mother and father and my brother and sister and my grandfather and two grandmothers outside Ningbo, which is a city near Shanghai. My father is a sailor so he is away a lot. When he is here he likes to cook. Mostly he cooks rice and vegetables. Because we live near the sea, we also eat a lot of fish. There are no sheep around here, but my grandfather has a pet monkey which he says tells him stories. My grandfather is a little bit crazy. He says some people in the west of the country eat monkeys, but I don't know if this is true.

Please tell me more about where you live. I have never been on a farm.
Yours,
Tomi Wong

When she had finished reading the letter, Shelley looked up to find Ms Garland standing before her.

"Did you like the letter?" Ms Garland asked.

"Yes," said Shelley, covering the page with her hands so that Ms Garland would not see that Tomi thought she still lived on a farm.

"And are you going to write back to him?" asked Ms Garland.

"Yes," said Shelley, and she sat there with her head down until Ms Garland went away.

# Chapter Four

The next day was Saturday, so Shelley and her mother went shopping in town. Because it was wet and they were tired, at lunch-time they went into a coffee shop for a rest. Shelley's mother started talking to a woman at the next table, so Shelley took out her copybook and wrote a second letter to Tomi Wong.

Meadow View
Tralee
County Kerry
Saturday 10th February


Dear Tomi Wong,

Thank you for your letter which was really great. Ningbo sounds like a lovely place to live, and it must be great to have your grandfather's monkey to play with.

Here on the farm . . .

She stopped and looked at her mother who was still talking to the other woman. Then she went back to the letter, crossed out the words Here on the farm and wrote instead:

Please write and tell me some more things about China and your family.
Yours,
Shelley Watters

When she was finished writing she looked up again and saw that her mother was ready to leave.

"Is that a letter to your new pen-pal?" said her mother, pointing to the copybook.

"Yes," said Shelley, but she turned the page quickly so that her mother wouldn't see what she had written.

## Chapter Five

On Monday morning, when she went back to school after the weekend, Shelley gave the new letter to Ms Garland.

"A second letter already?" said Ms Garland, looking at the sealed envelope with the words Tomi Wong on the outside. "Well done, Shelley."

Shelley tried very hard to look happy.

On Thursday morning Tomi Wong's reply arrived. Shelley took it down to the back of the classroom so that no one would see.

Ningbo
Zhejiang
China
Tuesday 13th February

Dear Shelley,

Thank you for your letter. I am sorry you did not tell me more about your life on the farm in Kerry, because I think it must be very interesting. At the moment I have a cold so I do not feel like writing very much. But next week I will write you a long letter about Ningbo.

Yours,
Tomi

When Ms Garland came down to see if everything was all right, Shelley knew it was time to show her the letter.

"Shelley," said Ms Garland, when she had read it through, "Tomi Wong seems to think you live in Kerry!"

"Yes, Miss," said Shelley. "It's where I used to live, before we moved to Dublin. I just thought it would be more interesting for someone living in China."

"In China!" exclaimed Ms Garland.

"Yes," said Shelley, pointing to the address at the top of Tomi's letter.

Ningbo
Zhejiang
China

"See? That's where he lives. Though I'm not sure I understand how his letters get here so quickly."

"Well," said Ms Garland, who was now looking very confused, "I'm not too sure myself. But why not write another letter now and tell him that you *used* to live in Kerry, but that *now* you live in Dublin? Then you'd be able to write about your friends and your school and where you live. I'm sure those things would be interesting to Tomi as well."

"Yes," said Shelley, glumly, "I suppose they would."

# Chapter Six

Over the next few days Shelley began a total of four letters – two each day! – but each time she was unhappy with them. For example, on Saturday she started to write a letter explaining that she really lived in Dublin with her mother in a small apartment, but then she got stuck again. She just couldn't think of anything to say.

The truth was that she didn't really have very many friends, so she couldn't write about what she did with them after school. Finally, the letter she gave to Ms Garland to send to Tomi simply read:

Meadow View
Tralee
County Kerry
Sunday 18th February

Dear Tomi,
I can't think of anything to write about at the moment. It is raining here. Tell me something more about Ningbo.
Bye.
Shelley

As usual Ms Garland took the letter; but this time she didn't ask Shelley anything about it, which made Shelley feel bad.

When Tomi's reply arrived the following Thursday morning, it made her feel even worse.

Ningbo
Zhejiang
China
Tuesday 20th February

Dear Shelley,

Do you live in a big farmhouse like the ones on TV? Do you have a car? In Ningbo most people go outside to do their exercise in the morning (the exercise is called t'ai chi and looks like a very slow dance). Then they cycle to work. Cycling is OK, however, because it does not rain here very much, except in July when the monsoon comes. Because my father is away at sea at the moment, my mother cycles with me to school and then she cycles to where she works in a newspaper office. What do your parents do? Do both of them work on the farm? After school I usually play table tennis with my friends. Then I eat with my family. My grandparents eat very slowly and then talk for hours and drink tea. My grandfather always talks about the mountains in the north where he grew up. Are there any mountains near you in Kerry?

Write back soon.

Yours,

Tomi

Shelley didn't know what to do. She waited until breaktime when all the other children were out in the school yard.

"Tell him the truth," Ms Garland suggested when Shelley showed her the letter. "It's always easier. The longer you go on pretending, the more difficult it will be in the end. And, anyway, the two of you already have a lot in common. Tomi's father is not living with him at the moment either. Maybe that would be a good thing to write about."

But Shelley didn't want to write about that.

Meadow View
Tralee
County Kerry
Thursday 22nd February

Dear Tomi,
The mountains around here are not really very big, but sometimes we go down to the MacGillycuddy's Reeks which are really very big.

When Shelley was beginning the second sentence of her reply, the pen just stopped moving in her hand.

Ms Garland was right. She couldn't write a letter like that. She couldn't pretend their messy flat in the city was really her dad's farmhouse in Kerry, and that there was a river just down the road and horses to go riding on.

All that was over now. It would be better not to write anything at all.

# Chapter Seven

That evening, when she had done her homework, Shelley went to her room and stared out the window on to the street. She was trying to think of something interesting to write about. She was really trying, but there wasn't anything: just people walking past in the rain, and traffic stopping at traffic-lights and then driving on.

"China is a fantastic place where it hardly ever rains, why would someone living there want to hear about a boring place like this?" she said to herself.

She got into bed and lay there unable to sleep. Suddenly, she knew the answer.

"Maybe he's never been in an Irish city!" she said aloud. "A city where all the signs are in English, and all the shops sell things he's probably never even seen!"

So, pretending she had never been in an Irish city herself, Shelley began to write about all the things she knew well as if she were seeing them for the first time.

In fact, there proved to be so many of them that she decided it would be easier to make a list.

1. The white lines that run down the middle of the street.

2. The yellow ones that run down along the sides.

3. The strange smells of cooking and different kinds of music outside the shops and restaurants as you pass by.

4. The different kinds of clothes people wear. Black suits, big coloured hats.

5. The different colours of people's skin...

She was still writing out her list when the pen slipped from her hand and she drifted off into a deep and comfortable sleep.

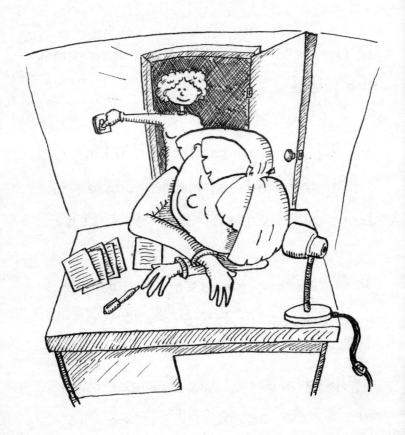

## Chapter Eight

"This is fantastic!" said Ms Garland the following morning when she saw the letter Shelley had finished after her breakfast. She was waving it over her head like the woman in the film did when she finished typing the last page of her book. She even insisted on reading the beginning of it aloud to the class.

Dear Tomi,

Actually I do not have my own chickens or sheep. The only chickens I know are on my dad's farm in the country, where I used to live, but I don't live there any more. Now I live in Dublin with my mother. There are a lot of people living on our street, but even though they pass up and down every day, most of them never really look at it. They are always too busy doing something else. For instance, I am probably the only person who knows how many parking meters there are on the street. (Parking meters are for parking your car.) 19 is the answer. I counted them. Maybe no one has ever counted them before, but I did. Because I wanted you to know all the things that are interesting about this street. In fact, here is a list of some of them...

"Shelley, this is a really great letter," said Ms Garland, flicking through the pages where Shelley had listed over one hundred interesting things on her street alone. "I think Tomi is going to be very excited to receive this."

But Shelley was barely listening. Someday, she was thinking to herself, someday she would write a whole book, like the woman in the film she had watched with her mother; a book so big she would need twenty shoe boxes to keep all of the words in.

That evening Shelley found the excitement of waiting for Tomi's reply almost too much to bear.

"I wrote and told him all about the street," she told her mother, who was reading an old magazine and drinking a cup of coffee.

"What street is that, Shelley?" asked her mother, looking up.

"Our street," said Shelley. She went over to the window and drew back the curtains. It was already dark outside. The lights of the apartment block opposite seemed to float against the blue-black sky.

Shelley's mother came over and stood beside her.

"Shelley, are you happy here?" she asked. "I know it's been difficult for you, moving away from your dad, coming to live in the city."

"Yes," said Shelley. "It was, at first. But I like it now. Now I'm learning to see the specialness of things."

"The what?" said her mother, surprised.

"The specialness," said Shelley. "Ms Garland says it's what you see at the start, when things are still new, but after a while they become sort of invisible and you have to look at them differently if you want to see it again."

"That's a beautiful idea, Shelley," said her mother, giving her a big hug.

"It's simple, really," said Shelley. "It's just that we forget."

## Chapter Nine

On Monday morning Shelley had decided to be first into class, but Ms Garland was already there when she arrived.

"Is there a letter for me today?" Shelley asked, full of excitement.

Ms Garland shook her head. "I'm afraid not," she said.

Shelley's heart sank.

"However," said Ms Garland, "there is something far better than a letter."

What could be better than a letter? Shelley wondered as Ms Garland opened the classroom door and in walked Mr Parris, one of the other teachers, with a small Chinese boy Shelley had seen around the school a couple of times before but had never talked to. In fact, she still hadn't figured it out when Ms Garland brought the boy over and introduced him.

"Shelley," she said, "I'd like you to meet
Tomi Wong. Tomi, this is Shelley."

"Hello," said Tomi Wong.

Shelley could hardly believe her eyes. Or her ears.

"All . . . all the way from China?" she finally managed to say. Tomi Wong looked a little embarrassed.

"Well, no, not exactly," said Ms Garland. "Actually Tomi lives in Alder Road, too. Isn't that right, Tomi?"

"Alder Road?" said Shelley. "But I thought . . ."

"Tomi moved here last year," Mr Parris said, "with his mother and father. But when he got your letter asking about China, he thought it would be more interesting for you to hear about what it's like over there."

"But that's why I pretended I was still living in Kerry!" said Shelley, turning to Ms Garland.

"There you are," said Ms Garland. "What did I tell you? You two already have a lot in common."

And with that, Ms Garland and Mr Parris stepped out into the corridor, leaving Shelley and Tomi staring silently at each other.

Outside they could hear the other children in the yard.

Finally Shelley said, "Do you want to go out and play?"

"I don't really know anyone to play with," said Tomi Wong, sadly.

"You know me!" said Shelley, which made Tomi smile. "You can play with me and tell me what you think about Ireland."

"OK," said Tomi Wong, and the two of them moved over to the door to go outside.

"And after that," said Shelley, "if you like, you can still tell me all about China."

# About the Author

Pat Boran was born in 1963 and currently lives in Dublin. He is a recipient of the Patrick Kavanagh Award for poetry and has published three collections of poems for adults, as well as a collection of short stories. He has conducted creative writing workshops in schools, colleges and with writing groups throughout the country and has had his stories and plays broadcast on RTE and BBC radio. He has been the editor of Poetry Ireland Review and reviews books for a number of newspapers and magazines. *All the Way from China* is his first book for children.

# About the Illustrator

Stewart Curry was born in 1976 and lives in Co Kildare. He is currently studying illustration in the National College of Art and Design in Dublin. His favourite colour is blue and he has a cat called Fluke. This is his first book to illustrate.